DOOMSDAY IN THE HEAVEN - PART (1)

VISAGE OF DOOMSDAY

ANMOL AGARWAL

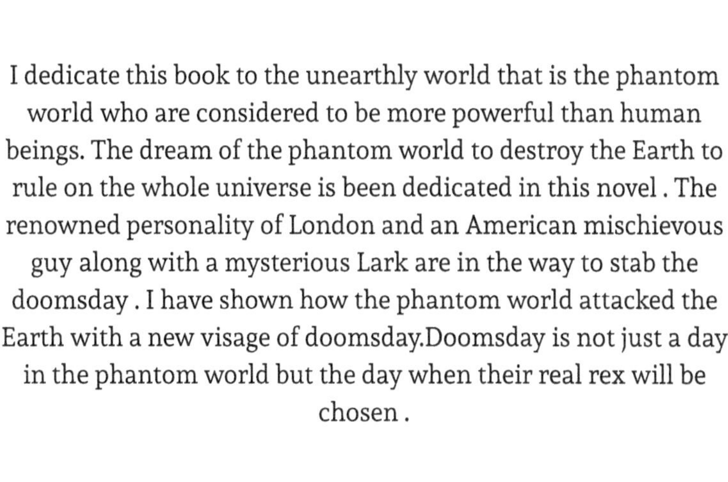

I dedicate this book to the unearthly world that is the phantom world who are considered to be more powerful than human beings. The dream of the phantom world to destroy the Earth to rule on the whole universe is been dedicated in this novel . The renowned personality of London and an American mischievous guy along with a mysterious Lark are in the way to stab the doomsday . I have shown how the phantom world attacked the Earth with a new visage of doomsday.Doomsday is not just a day in the phantom world but the day when their real rex will be chosen .

Contents

Preface

I, Anmol Agarwal , wrote this novel ' DOOMSDAY IN TH HEAVEN '
, which is divided in two parts ,to let any living beings understand
that there are some other species or unearthly bodies which are
more powerful than us that even they can devastate the whole Earth
,as described in the novel .Usually the way Mr. Brayden was chosen
the person as a culprit and salve of doomsday iterates the
importance given to the person despite he has done a dingy wrong
which he considered macabre in his past . The doomsday by
phantom world is quiet new to experience and the real visage is
still out of reach to any of the character of the novel .The way Mr.
Brayden , whom others considered a person with swift and candid
mind finds the solution to cease doomsday created by the phanto
world.

Acknowledgements

I thank to all those who make my task fulfill by reading this novel .I thank to all those also who literally helped me to write this novel .I hope you all will like the sketches and characters of the novel .

THANKING YOU,

ANMOL AGARWAL

Prologue

The story begins with the Last day of London of Mr. Brayden as he wanted to leave London due to his macabre and dingy wrong . He was a character full of personality always wanting the things to happen as he wishes to happen .He met with a jolly guy in the train who tried to cheat Mr.Brayden . He made him his true friend and took the trip to Switzerland .They found a speaking lark in the train to whom they also involved in their group. Their first day in Switzerland proved mysterious .Lets see how they elapsed their days in Switzerland , a new country to both the novel passengers .

1

LASTDAY IN LONDON

Due to the dingy wrong, Mark Brayden, one of the well known personality of London, padlocked his palatial yard and beat around the bush. The macabre wrong that had choken his heart incessantly perturbed him and to recover from his bad deeds, he had forsaken his charming yard and left for the London Underground.

The undying belt of dazzle rapped and rattled the stout windows of his fancied house in the heart of London. The flux of intrepid air purged the garb and grappled the dainty colours in the house of Mr. Brayden. The vent waived the infirm griefs of the queer abode. The posh plumages of his abode could feel the profound emotions of the immense pitcher. The temper of the terrific mansion relied on the twitters of people, loud gusts of gabs and jest.

Without mirth, the fog of murk fades the spick heart of the paradise. People often call the house of Mark Brayden **'THE MANSE OF UNDYING UPROARS'**.

On the demise of the mansion, the godforsaken air inside it gasps due to the ghastly conditions and the horror deuce of darkness convulses the yard in a grisly way.The strange ghost regulates the mansion residing in its mind.

Mr Brayden , a great hero altered the sufferings of people of London, delued the heart of the yard , but unfortunately he had found nothing. Being an extremely adept and acute sensitive guy, he used to perplex people with the use of mysterious words to affix situations with some interest. Any apt and ardent adventure from a flourishing arcade to refreshing air has not subdued him from challenging the struggles of life. Only dread of Mr Brayden's life was to scare. His rarity was that he always wanted things to go as he wishes to happen. One of the jolly incident of Mr. Brayden's life happened in his childhood. Once in younger times, his rude teacher erased the blackboard but left some part of it deliberately.This started itching in the mind of Mr Brayden and he stood up from the bench and erased the left part. The attentive eyes were glaring him for disturbing the class with his odd jobs.

Mr Brayden was a man of innocent look. He usually expatiated his feelings and the ethos to others. His actions sometimes created hilarious situations and often led to circumstances also. His only volition is to know the world. And to fulfill his dreams, he became an intelligent engineer, a sincere doctor and a desiring teacher and now eventually working as a detective for the world. His this profession prompted him to travel around the world as he had already traversed over 35 countries . In this arena of job, he spent only some months after completion of his task of a detective in most of the countries . But was living in London from many months just like London city and its citizens touched Mr. Brayden's heart that he was coercing to smash the sombre kindred that had initiated his every morning with an inkling of sobriety and had impelled him at every aspect of his life.

The ache beseiged the blaze of the London city and became indecent blemish in London. The departure of Mr. Brayden infused apprehension and sadness in the ideal minds of Londoners. They reminisced Mr. Brayden as a guy full of patience and contentment with his jobs. But today they are not satiated with his fatuous work to leave thier city.

Mr Brayden had curtailed the sufferings of the poor and performed various jobs to provide food and clothings to them. And to illuminate all these immense aids of Mr. Brayden, the people of London gathered near the London Underground and created a vehement pageant . This impromptu gusto of Mr. Brayden defined that any wicked person had brain washed him. Mr.Brayden's huge heart consigned his all repast and grandeur to his stalwart kiths. The travail in London city of Mr. Brayden produced the splendour from the gracious hearts of Londoners. His mettle altered London into a city of dreams. The people of London shouted to ask Mr. Brayden the wrong they had committed that he was punishing them in that way.

Mr. Mark Brayden assured to idealise the Londoners,

"Bare to tell my bluds.

It's not your deeds forcing me to light the lamp of another city in my brain and nor anyone brain washed me. Don't take this claim on your heads.

It is only me who had done something wrong which is even not forgiven by any. "

Again everyone shouted that the beautiful gem of an extremely pretty necklace broken to loss all the shining of it.

Mr Brayden remarked ,

"When the tunes of air link the garms of London to our youngers, then our coronary smile becomes the pomade for the flourising city of London. And that ripping air is here with you!

When the dred barb and ragged faces of rapacious people had jacked the firm reputation of the citizens of London city, the nymph of the city strove to achieve the paramount heyday from the wicked people in the world. And that overwhelming and ever shining heyday is with you!

When the safe cheeks find a pampered fam and soil, their modest visage will always rattle the door of victory. And that divine child has born in London!

My imperceptible harangue has hit the sack and my din has strained to entrap the benedictions from my elders and has bewared the youngers from the marshes of anxiety. "

The last words of Mr. Mark Brayden altered the minds of the people of London. Persuaded by his talking , they were ready to concede that thier city was filled with prowess. De facto, Dwindling the fame of Esquire Brayden will impeach their country. Mr. Mark Brayden stowwed his legs in the train giving a cur of obeisance and blessed the people, 'Break a leg!'.

The vivacious soul of London did a venture and flittered and fluttered and again became strong.

2

JOURNEY IN THE TRAIN

Waiving the credible air and people of London, Mr. Mark Brayden stowwed his legs on the train. The train absconded at eight p.m. abruptly. Regressing several stations, the train would reach Switzerland, the place where Mr. Brayden was willing to derail. He has not ascribed the idea of going to Switzerland not even to his wellwishers.Mr. Brayden was good at digesting the secrets that even the Almighty falters to seek the truth.

Enter Caption

The aisle of the train was very crowded. The travellers were hustling to others and jerking the train with their malignant sound. The lunatics were dancing on the berth and ramming the shrewd men in a sheepish way. The people were juxtaposed as it seemed the scabbard did not have rambunctious space to sheathe a sword. Every knack was kindled for the seat. Frisking children was grasped to be tolerated but crowd got fretted when an insane man along with his group somersaulted to seek some space in the congested train. After that , crowd resolved only toilet the handsome space provided to the circus group. Thier fury crumbled when a berth was seen vacant and everyone attacked on it.But the enormous sea was still huge after empting one fist of water from the boundless sea.

The struggle in the train was constricted into a gist by Mr. Brayden,

Not curbed the crowd ,it's roots,

Not regulated the crowd ,it's branches,

It's leaves were much as flotant,

Crowd as a tree dances, not stagnant.

Mr. Brayden flustered to see the crowd and flitted in it. He felt he was crumbled with the unanonymous crowd and his crumbs would be crumpled in this war. Every corners were attacked and pounced due to the extreme paucity of space.

The sizzle of the congestion thumped Mr. Brayden and one of the lunatics quashed the boots of Mr. Lenvo, one of the traveller. The pair of boots left ragged and useless after being crushed by a mad. Mr. Lenvo, a journalist , prattled, " My twenty nine dollars boots! My extra expensive boots from Japan! This putrid crowd and one of its absurd men pecked my boots!"

Mr. Lenvo , the egoist, caught Mr. Brayden as a culprit and said, "Hey ! Listen fatuous man! You have quashed my boots in this congestion".

Handling the situation, Mr. Brayden commended , " Hey brother! You are one of the those fools who have been packed in the toilet by the crowd ".

Mr. Brayden vexed him and smiled at him. Mr. Lenvo, almost sank in the pool of anger , condemned Mr. Brayden, " Clutch your dirty tongue! That was not me! Sincerely accept your mistake ".

Mr. Brayden confided, "Brother! Pardon but God knows I have not clashed your foolproof boots".

Mr. Lenvo, burnt in the fire of revenge, shouted , " What you said? Foolproof boot!" and exonerated," Garrulous, it costs fifty five dollars. You must have to pay me ".

Mr. Lenvo was known to be a hostile guy but self centered. Quiet a conceit person due to his richness, he left several multinational companies professing all of them only fag and many jobs in school. The travesty of Mr. Lenvo had produced various harmful consequences which had prompted several principals and teachers to abdicate due to his madness and twit character. Eventually he became journalist and still working as an agent in the ' The London Times' and today traversing to Switzerland to cook some fresh news .His haughty and unbridled life had abided many disgraces from corners of the world.

Mr. Lenvo was ready to earn the payment from Mr. Brayden. Mr. Brayden assured him, " Cease your tosh! I have not clashed your boots then why should I pay you fifty five dollars.The hideous crowd has already constipated my feeble legs and it is swaying them the way it wants".

Mr. Lenvo again flaunted, " Queer person, Your mistake costs one hundred and ten dollars inasmuch as I said only a single boot costs fifty five dollars". He comprehended Mr. Brayden a decorous and pertinent person to befool and persecute him by asking his payment of one hundred and ten dollars. But the pervasive Brayden had grasped Mr. Lenvo's drama. He replied, " Your dudgeon".

The cheated rays of voice of Mr. Lenvo enkindled the sound of Mr. Brayden. The dullard resurrected in a loud sound, " Do not be so cheap, tyrant! I only speak to branded mouths! Much disparities reside between I ,the rich , and you, the poor. As fast as you can pay me my dollars Otherwise ".He stopped by saying this much and gave an ultimatum to Mr. Brayden to pay or he had to choose any other way to get the payment.

Irate Mr. Brayden also had profess experience with such lunatics and their befooling tactics. He also sought the same way to get rid of the wrong conviction sealed on him by Mr. Lenvo. He forbore much and exaggerated to Mr. Lenvo, "Doesn't matter your ears listen only to branded mouths.

Doesn't matter your mouth jabbers about your own richness.

But definitely your eyes are still weak to recognise the commensurate personality of any person" and added that " I am the utmost businessman of London . You are not much aware of my earnings of millions per day. You have ruined my few minutes in which I could have earned thousands of dollars. And you have wasted all that. "

Mr. Lenvo shocked to hear about the glory of Mr. Brayden whom he considered a culprit and penniless.

Mr. Brayden said in a low voice but still energetic, " You must have to pay in thousands to me for the time you have wasted. Scarify your heart and give me my dollars. "

The trumpeting of elephant ravaged the bleating of goat. Mr. Lenvo can even crucify his grandeur but can't consign a single penny to anyone .He was submerged in the air of desperation when Mr. Brayden in whose web he was trapped and considered much richer than himself , asked for his payment.

3

ARRIVAL OF THE LARK

The ignoble man prayed to the rich personality to ask for anything but leave his heart. Captious God comprehended the evil that had ruined the character of Mr. Lenvo. He chastised his crook ," I only want the prickle of your life not your dollars nor even your spick boots but just your pitiless flaw and idle attitude to your penny .Crumble your coxcomb nature and stubborn attitude towards your money and grandeur. Be a light hearted guy! "

Mr. Lenvo was much lured with Mr. Brayden's traquil and venial character. He commenced opting him very much and left his obdurate and garrulous life. The flamboyant springe heard a squall and shattered the attitude of Mr. Lenvo. Exulting after altering an unfeasible job to make feasible, Mr. Brayden found a new companion in his journey to the eternity of world and evaded him from the wrong path of life. Though Mr. Brayden condoned him and Mr. Lenvo modified to a pious of Mr. Brayden but he has not left his jeering and fickle nature.

The train persevered very long despite of enormous multitude. But the first station was not much far to bless the train . The first station at last arrived vitalizing many passengers. The train was reconditioned there. Peculiar vista of calm and vacuous country glistened every grim visage of travellers. Past incursion in train seemed again when the same attack took at the first station when everyone was trying to derail at once horridly and infuriated each other. What type of unison is this among people!

The train was enough vacant after the first station that at least seats were available for those who had paid for that. Switzerland, where both the guys were willing to go ,was the third station . Both the gracious friends became laid-back and crouched on the berth with a loud sigh of relief. The relief was of their grisly contention in the cul-de-sac of the studious train.

Finally, Suave Mr. Brayden confessed Mr. Lenvo that he was not any businessman nor any rich personality. Inspite of it , Mr. Lenvo, who was an American , did not recede doing true reliance on his sir, Mr. Brayden.After revealing this, Mr. Brayden verged in front of Mr. Lenvo and felt sigh when he told him that he had committed an extremely paltry mistake. When jittery Mr. Lenvo tried to know about the mistake and why Mr. Brayden resolved for Switzerland, then he told that he could not tell him anything at that time and would reveal the whole history some time in the future. To stifle the obscure time , Mr. Lenvo commenced some different gab so to take away the awful mind of Mr. Brayden . Both the spruce men relished the savour of each other by totally being absorbed in the gab.

Suddenly, abroad the train, the pervading calmness was fritterred with a loud din and burgled every ears. Declaiming the gist of life, the cryptic din embellished the torment of the train. The twitterring tone trampled the tranquility of the train. Indeed, it depraved the humble hearts of the travellers .The man who has just started living a good life was shocked and enquired to Mr. Brayden, " Expunging the pacified time from outskirts , what is this that is disturbing the evergreen calmness? "Mr.Brayden deplored, " Perhaps, the ubiquitous ding-dongs perk the quiescent temples in the sleepy dawn to remind Almighty about it's obligations or the decorous men are quelling the peculiar spirit by singing a smearing dirge".Everyone grasped that the din was not a jest but an irrevocable intruder. It became perpetual, whispering and whizzing in the morose minds of Mr. Brayden and other train-travellers.

Shattering the glass of the window, a progeny of parrot penetrated and shrouded under the fallow hand of Mr. Brayden. It's legs were paining as a prong had been stuck in them. The travellers amazed to see a fascinating and flamboyant lark which had already dazed them. After groped in the hands of Mr. Brayden, the dainty lark squealed and shrieked from sultry pang. It's expectations of aids. from Mr. Brayden proved true when Mr. Brayden deadened the personable lark by plucking the prong. Fondly, the vibrant lark dilated a gust of delight and lilted a doleful tone dropping the rapture . It's voice was extremely sweet to ears and ravished almost all the travellers.The glistening quill of wavering lark memorized the mild and scarlet flowers with some deceived bows of umber. The fuzzy feathers of the lark glimmered the air and initiated wagging to secede from the hands of Mr. Brayden. It's haggard head flared the shine of the gloss.

The gravitating neck of lark twittered and incautious clouds abruptly tumbled to see it's glory. Puny it was but could entangle the pitcher enmasse in it's profuse and fervent beauty. The intent smile of the fickle progeny clenched the bloods of people in a long chain symbolising their unison. Immediate arrival of lark and sudden departure of apprehensions painted a gaiety climate using a wand.

The lark after roaming the whole train sat on the ample hands of Mr. Brayden, airing an affluent relationship with him.

The ingenuous arrival of the progeny warped the train from a peevish to a vacuous one. Between this wee sobriety ,the fictitious progeny twittered , "My jolly heart thanks you the souvenir of generosity on this mother Earth".The talking lark became the tidings in the train from one compartment to another. The unwitting thrush pelted the demure travellers with its quelling voice. Since almost all the travellers in the train had not heard a lark speaking with much efficiency so several prospects and perceptions aired regarding the abrupt arrival of a mysterious lark . Mr. Brayden's restless eyes hobbled in the train and started glittering with a long sight of the progeny.

Lark became the forefront of gabs of Mr. Brayden and all other travellers in the train. Everyone was perplexed whether to recognise the obsolete progeny a gift from providence or an occult merchandise of eternal nature.

4

ADVENTURES OF MR. LENVO

The speaking lark wreathed a suspicious idea in the minds of the travellers. Mr. Lenvo was not much astonished with this mysterious lark. He refunded Mr. Brayden , " Why are your rheumy eyes perceiving the Lark , that it seems they have seen such a Lark first time in their life" . Mr. Brayden almost raptured in the beauty and voice of Lark commentated, " The vista of such a quaint Lark vitalized the way to prune the prosy thickets of life. It's charming sound promulgates the essence of heaven and its peerless habiliments impel onlookers to ravish in the beauty of dainty feathers " and investigated, "Brother Lenvo! Have you ever seen such a queer Lark under the precincts of the Earth ? "

First time it was in his life, when Mr. Lenvo was provided voice to untangle the truth . Peal of the guttural sound of Mr. Lenvo reechoed in the comparment of the train. He propitiated to the audience who was eager to listen him, " Few days elapsed when I was planning to invite my voracious friends and finally clinched of a trip to zoo. My plan was to invite them in the nearby zoo first and after that I will scare them with my guise of an ape and extraordinary acting. For that I chose a vile zoo for the trip as I thought why to become much lavish and expand my expenses for my barbaric friends.Since my outstanding plan was cooked, only what was left to stand perfect in it ".

The train travellers were waiting the main climax but Mr. Lenvo was relished with his history and reaffirmed, " The day came when I asked my friends for the trip to zoo. My costume of a ghastly ape was also ready. After few hours in the zoo, I saw a lark iterating to an ape. But unlike it, the ape was mute and firmly listened to the Lark who told it that no human ears could be able to hear it's occult heart. The Lark finally hushed and I , an inert, has not given much attention on that fact because it was high time to scare my friends with my horrendous garb " and he gabbled, "But my plan was totally failed when I was unable to find my guise, which I had bought of several dollars ,of the ape . It seemed someone had stolen it the time when I was with my friends. My dollars...".

The travellers were almost in tears for not the wasted dollars of Mr. Lenvo but for the time they has wasted by enquiring to him. Mr. Brayden ,tired from the useless grouching of Mr. Lenvo , burbled ," Huge request garrulous! Rest your tongue! Don't prompt my hideous mind to plan to cease it for days". The requisite arrow from the bow of Mr. Brayden stuck in the mouth of Mr. Lenvo . Eventually, the rancid talks of the peevish Lenvo were slain . The train was placated.

The conspicuous beauty of the Lark touched the apex. Leaving behind all the mysteries regarding the speaking Lark, the detective who was blessed by the travellers for stopping the mouth of Mr. Lenvo baptised it, Flen and ravished in taking the taste of it.

Mr. Brayden disregarded the obscene and futile talks of Mr. Lenvo. But Mr. Lenvo was ready to bore the train with his odd gabs. He captured a victim and mumbled an elegy with the acting of a dare devil, "Don't you know my friend what was happened with me one night? "

The victim ignored him replying , " Sorry! I don't want to talk to you ".

Mr. Lenvo continued, "When I went to sleep at midnight, then suddenly I heard a loud neigh of horse . It was frequently reechoing in my ears. I ,with much fear in my heart , woke and wandered in search of the source. The onset was much horrid and it became even more horrendous when I saw an extremely bright stone near a moor. My daring heart permeated a ghastly moonlight. I went their slowly and was shocked to see the stone. Do you know what it was, my companion? "

Now, the victim was also in mood and answered, "Confirmation iterates that it would be any mysterious stone that had been splattered from the sky ".

Mr. Lenvo enveloped the train in a curtain of mysticism and confessed," Wrong, It was not any mysterious stone but some sparse dollars on the ground . But I had not taken it ".

The untoward victim of Mr. Lenvo raged and asked why he had not taken it since he always had the appetite of dollars. Mr. Lenvo modified his guttural sound and grumbled, " Because after some time I came to know that it was not even real, I was just dreaming and saw a nightmare. And all this happened twelve years past. I always have felt remorse for not taking the dollars".

Mr. Lenvo tinkled and commenced weeping for the dollars he had lost in the nightmare. The victim was rampaged and shouted with a thunder at Mr. Lenvo, "Hobo! Insane! Your irritating voice has devastated my ears. Rogue! It will be much better to give you money than to hark your ignoble elegy".

Sobreity reigned a span. Flen slept under the vacant hands of Mr. Brayden. Mr. Brayden was rebuking Mr. Lenvo for his ill habits.Being tired from travelling and chiding him, Mr. Brayden left the rest scoldings for future.

The proximate station quaered the victims whether they would opt to get rid of Mr. Lenvo. Those travellers who had paid for Switzerland also derailed due to the daunting voice of Mr. Lenvo.

The climate was flourished with the pervading puff of the nature whose heart was incessantly pulsating to provide fresh air to its children. From its huge pelf, it has felled pails of water from clouds to beatify the pitcher with the plentitude of merciness. The whole world was blessed with the cascades of rain that has created a demure surrounding.

5

THE TIDINGS OF DOOMSDAY

The train started its journey once again leaving the station behind. Since the audacity among the travellers was lost to travel more with Mr. Lenvo so all of them derailed in the second station. After it, the train was left with only six travellers : Mr. Brayden who has just scolded Mr. Lenvo for his restive behaviour, Flen , Mr. Lenvo the culprit of the vacant train, the sobriety which purged the train, a newspaper which was seized by Mr. Lenvo from an old to read and finally the dollars which the victim who was outraged by Mr. Lenvo left for Lenvo's medical check-up.

The land of Switzerland was very long to reach. The errant weather reanimated with the dried leaves of sun and the sporadic calmness adorned the illustrious grove. Entangling the squalor of the nature in the stern cobwebs with it's straps, the pure soul of the nature vanished it in the boundless universe. Mangling the darkness of clouds , the lucrative rays of the Sun glowed each helm of the Earth. It has infused hypnotism among the dwellers .Profuse snow oozed from the far peaks and sunflowers wagged in whim under the hills giving them a panoramic vista.

Crossing all the obstacles, the train cherished all the steadfast view and kept planting towards it's destiny. Since all the travellers had already derailed except some of them, Mr. Brayden reposed few minutes and initiated reading the stolen newspaper assuming a prolonged sobriety in the trail. Flen was still sleeping or might be acting so to evade itself from the wary eyes of Mr. Lenvo. Mr. Lenvo was disgruntled and adopted some dignity in his mind. He started planning for a trip to Paris utilizing the dollars left by the victim.

Mr. Brayden sidetracked , " Brother Lenvo ! What work prompted you to travel to Switzerland? "

Mr. Lenvo solemnly answered , " Actually I am a journalist and my boss has heard about the upcoming doomsday and he was mesmerized with this tidings . He wanted his agents to be omnipresent and report the freshly cooked news. But I am not going to stand perfect in this idea as from my vision, doomsday is just a misconception. And these types of updates will only promote misconstring of this rumour among the innocents. "

Praising the idea and decision of Mr. Lenvo, Mr. Brayden quothed while reading the newspaper,

"....EVEN THE SHROUDS WILL RUMBLE ON STRIKEN BY DOOMSDAY ....

This showy and stern headline will shove the pitcher in the fire of demise. The description illustrates that the horrific doomsday will definitely lead to crowds stampede on the roads amputating the legs and hands of them.It will rip the belly of people and suck their quivering arteries as a vampire. Several lives will be crucified. The streak of the firm sky will get stooped under the soil of the mother Earth. This indestructible havoc will inate the oceans to submerge the whole Earth and blood will be flowed from the painful eyes of the sterile humans. This invincible intrigue of God Almighty will burst the clouds which will rain acids in the life of the stagnant people and instigate the fire in the volcanoes. Eventually, the ferved fire will devise to burn the writhing entity of the world leaving only the sultry climate with profess black fumes and stuffy air.

James Whitacher, an exquisite seer has foreseen the horoscope of Earth and proclaimed a terrified doomsday in the mid month of July this year.

This mad seer is horrifying the whole pitcher with his wrong prophecy of an upcoming dreadful doomsday".

Mr. Brayden took a sigh of relief after quothing the whole news. Mr. Lenvo desperated on the ghastly description and commented, "Right sir! The insane seer is deluding the whole world by announcing that he had googled the future time and foretold the fortune of the Earth by studing the positions of the fickle planets and wagging stars. And the bad news is that most of the people have initiated trusting on this rumour spread by the seer who has frightened the world ".

Mr. Brayden told that the seer had to be imprisoned for scaring the world with his formidable horoscope. Mr. Lenvo nodded with the idea of Mr. Brayden. Flen woke up after meeting a sweet sleep. Emulating from the supportive hands of Mr. Brayden, it heeded on the situation .

Mr. Lenvo cogitated and found this the best time to know more about Flen. In the premonition of being bored by Mr. Lenvo, Flen commenced roaming in the compartments of the train. Mr. Brayden also felt tired and resolved to sleep for some time. Mr. Lenvo pursued Flen and finally reached in the compartment of the loco pilot and started prodding him.

The weather outside relinquished the glistening sunshine by evicting the handy sun rays . The Sun perpetuated his prayers in the humble hearts of people and now the Moon imbibed the chance to ajar the hoard of happiness for the dwellers of Earth. The twinkling stars jutted reincarnating the whole climate with their colossal glow . The plop of the overflowing river filled every potholes on the ground mingling a tint of merriness in water and quenched the parched pitcher. Loud sound of the paces of quelling air paced and reverberated in the surroundings.

The new Sun fostered once again.

Mr. Brayden after waking up from a long sleep saw Mr. Lenvo fallen from his seat. Not able to find his pet Lark ,he questioned himself about the place where it was dwelling. He awoke Mr. Lenvo but his wary eyes were only searching it. Abruptly, Flen arrived and confided that it was just absorbing the dainty vista of climate and was wandering in the compartments of the train.

Switzerland was only an hour to reach. Mr. Lenvo asked Mr. Brayden, " Sir! Not much distance is left to the destination. Do you have any plans cooked in your mind where to reside in Switzerland since I have already left my job of journalist by not investigating on the upcoming doomsday? "

Mr. Brayden answered negatively with a dismal face.

6

MYSTERIOUS DAY IN SWITZERLAND

The time was not ridiculous. The forlorn reply from Mr. Brayden strewed the boundless affliction in the train since the life was not decided yet in Switzerland. Exterminating it's long trip , the train at last honked in Switzerland rambling the path of bliss and grief .The fascinating hoar hue of the clouds pared the murk of the picturesque sky.

The train arrived at the station at nine p.m. Mr. Brayden and his companions astonished with the smug beauty of thier destiny. With some struts in arms and waist, Mr. Brayden derailed and was pleased from the dainty climate of Switzerland. Snow falling perennially enriched the shine of the country. The three travellers were perked with the charming climate which has induced them to settle in the unwitting place. They all toddled in the rain of ice trembling from cold. The paucity of fire cushioned when Flen sought some alone firewoods burning near the nook of a snow-covered house.

Icicles as jubilant love jingle the rain on the vague thresholds with some loud peals of plop. There was a pram which creaked a lot paring the dazzle of the country. The sobriety was perpetuated in the climate that every ticking of the belfry echoed in the calm surroundings. During this austere time of vagabonds, their every penance in search of an inn altered into a botch. Mr. Brayden along with his gang flounced in the new country pleading every Swiss to lend accommodation. But no one was ready to relent on their piteous conditions .Mr. Brayden was afflicted even more when everyone denied to provide a room to a stranger.

The sunshine fainted in the life of travellers with the setting of Sun . The night sky seemed nought obliterating every shine in the fortune of migrators. Vacillating on the whizzed path at night, the zoic vagrants were awaiting the next cooing of the cock as it might reform the wilderness of their life to a fruitful grove. Until then, they acceded their wretched faith.

Both friends, Mr. Brayden and Mr. Lenvo were tired of roaming and finally slept under the calm shade of a tree. Flen was also feeling tiredness and slept on the tree.

The new day rose with the Sun.

The clucks of hen aroused Mr. Brayden. Mr. Lenvo and Flen were still in sweet dreams. Mr. Brayden was still dithered about the nature of Swiss why they were hesitating to lend an inn. He saw a greengrocer on the footpath with his pushcart full of vegetables. The idea to ask him the reason for that evoked in the mind of Mr. Brayden and he stood and stopped the greengrocer.

Mr. Brayden enquired , " Good morning friend! May I ask you something? "The greengrocer showed his hospitality and allowed Mr. Brayden to ask.

Mr. Brayden enquired pointing Mr. Lenvo, " Actually we are new to this country. And we want some accommodation but no Swiss showed humanity towards us and not provided any room.... "

The intelligent greengrocer grasped what Mr. Brayden wanted to ask. He confided him, " Friend! I can understand what you want to ask that why no one is ready to accommodate you. The truth is that the mind of the people of Switzerland is congested with the fear of the upcoming doomsday. A pernicious rumour has wiped out the ingenious mind of Swiss . It is echoing in the whole land of Switzerland passing from mind to mind. The people of Switzerland has thought that a malign pestilence in the name of doomsday will abrade the whole pitcher. Victims will wriggle in their abode much that the streams of blood will be flowed from their body but no vaccine can ameliorate the withered breaths. Neither the talisman can work nor the wits of Lords can save the world. Just a puff by providence and pestilence will definitely perish the existence of humanity on the Earth with its outrage and quench the parched world with the veins of humans. The fierce fire will leave mere the ashes of sobriety which will outlive after this obsolete pestilence".

In the middle of the conversation , Mr. Brayden was scared when Mr. Lenvo placed his one hand on his shoulder asking him what the greengrocer was talking about.

Mr. Brayden took a sign of relief and replied, " Oh! It's you Mr. Lenvo!
"

Mr. Brayden summarised the whole rumour to Mr. Lenvo. But still perplexed Brayden asked the greengrocer why then the people of Switzerland were not providing any space to them "?

The greengrocer confided , " Actually, their is a person who has pervaded the rumour. And that guy has spread it with the idea that a foreigner will ravage the whole country by transmitting the germs to Swiss. So the people of Switzerland has resolved to evade from the ghastly pestilence by not accommodating foreigners in their house. This foolishness has planted a xenophobia for the foreigners among the people of Switzerland .This has prompted every Swiss not to accommodate any foreigner".

Mr. Lenvo asked the greengrocer about that person who had pervaded that rumour in Switzerland .

The greengrocer answered that he was not aware of that guy.

Mr. Brayden trembled listening the weird mind of the miscreant and told that that guy had spread the rumour among Swiss to ruin the whole country and create a sense of terror for foreigners. Mr. Lenvo thanked the greengrocer and the latter welcomed leaving for his work. Mr. Brayden said with a gaudy sound," The goading of that foolish person has horrified the people of Switzerland ".

Mr. Lenvo replied positively.

Nullifying the obscure prophecy of pestilence, Mr. Brayden along with his two comrades were in the way to leave the country for there will be noone to lend a helping hand.

The alpine rays of the Sun owed the lands of Switzerland. On the weary path, Mr. Brayden with his two rogues ambled and was only few miles far to reach the borders of Switzerland. Their desperate eyes were only exploring a place to stay and smite their hunger. Suddenly, it seemed Mr. Brayden's struggle in London proved fruitful and the three wanderers found a lonely house.

7

IN THE TERRIBLE HOUSE

Mr. Lenvo iterated, " It seems the God Almighty heard our prayers ". Mr. Brayden replied, " May be! But firstly we must go inside the house to talk to its owner ".

Their was a hoarding full of dirt and filth hung on the lonely house . Something anonymous was written on it "

DRAY'S T. M. U. U. ". Mr. Brayden surmised on the dirty hoarding and the mysterious words written on it .The gruesome picture of a strange lonely house with an obsolete hoarding painted a tint of suspicion in the swift mind of the detective.

The gasping air of the house symbolised that it was there from many years. Throbs of the house were dwindling but the spirit had firmly resided in its heart. Encircled with the cypress trees, the rustic house was alone there reposing far away from the sufferings of town. Ripping the steadfast leaves of trees, the sparkling rays of the Sun splattered pouring the pool of tranquility on the old house. The tremendous house reminisced that a mystery was hidden inside it. It's unique name and moreover , it's eccentric outside infrastructure horrified a lot to individuals.

The mood of the weather changed as the three travellers ascended towards the house. Vacuous shine of the milky clouds scurried with the gurgles of black clouds . The itinerant air aired with sand and dust overlapping the vista of the house. Hemming trees swayed swiftly with the air and the rustling of leaves frightened the wanderers .

Mr. Brayden kept Flen in his pocket. Both the friends ran quickly towards the hotel. Finally the three souls landed on the platform of the old house. The whirlwind outside almost convulsed and disarrayed the whole house.

Mr. Lenvo opened the dilapidated door of the queer house and startled after having the glance of it. Pails of dust were poured in the glade like fallow hall of the house where the snarling of the dark clouds was reverberating. Ruptures of the rugged wooden stairs seemed boundless and it's appalling exit ended opening the path to hell. Wiggling windows of the rooms abetted the widespread fright around. The sheer mysteries hidden in the nooks of the world seceded from the cobwebs of conjurers and roved in this house. The messed rooms, the wobbling chairs and the grunting vespiary illuminated that the house was standing posthumously.

A horrid feeling in the heart of Mr. Brayden pealed to reject the abominable house of frightening look. Mr. Lenvo grasped what Mr. Brayden was thinking gazing his irrevocable and scared eyes. But, he overhauled Mr. Brayden by convincing his cumbersome heart about the lack of any other roof for shade and eventually persuaded him to reside there due to their awful compulsion under the confines of Switzerland.

The weather was meliorated outside. Motley sky marred the fiend of climate and the fledged birds commenced twittering in the graceful air.

Mr. Lenvo with Mr. Brayden and the lark were reposing in one of the rooms of the ancient house. Mr. Brayden iterated that no one might reside in that old house then. Mr. Lenvo replied, " May be ! "

Immediately the weary lamps of the room ceased glowing and darkness ruined the morale of Mr. Lenvo. He screamed loudly in fear and fell from the bed. Mr. Brayden aroused dizzy Lenvo who was almost fainted with terror and screamed, " Wake up brother! Look! Who is there "!

The lamps again enlightened the room .A fat and nimble shadow ascended in the room drizzling affright in the room. Eventually, the man entered in the room and astonished to see all of them. Frightened Lenvo circled his hands against the chest of Mr. Brayden and asked, " Who are you "? The men quothed , "What! Why are you asking this? Despite , I should ask this question to you. Well, I am the owner of this abode, Mr. William Forge ".

Mr. Brayden doodled the whole history to Mr. Forge related to their life and the struggles and circumstances they had faced before reaching there. He pleaded Mr. Forge to provide accommodation to the wanderers and he also avouched him that he would work hard and pay his rents .

Mr. Forge grasped that Mr. Brayden was a kind hearted person and lent his house. But he refused to take the rents from Mr. Brayden.But this ruined the self-respect of Mr. Brayden and he forcibly convinced Mr. Forge for the rents. Mr. Forge was an authentic and pragmatic man with a magnanimous heart. He was very old to perform jobs. Only few years elapsed when he was also one of the trustee of Switzerland as his contention to meliorate the country utilising his swift intellect was really meritorious. But his life was totally altered due to an outrageous tragedy.

Mr. Forge was a gracious person. He braced the three wishy washy travellers : Mr.Brayden , Mr. Lenvo and the lark, FlenFlen in his house. Flen usually roamed around the sky flying high with its noval group or sometimes also played with Mr. Lenvo. Being a novice in the country, Mr. Brayden found various difficulties to get selected for any job. Eventually, he was rendered a job of prospecting freshly cooked news in the country. He got employed there. But the useless Lenvo has ransacked various vacancies. If he somewhat joined in any of the agencies ,then he was unable to comprehend the work there offhand and finally left the job. He was still left unemployed.

Days elapsed and the month of February arrived. Mr. Forge trusted Mr. Brayden too much and with this reliability, he commenced sharing his privies of his old grandeur with Mr. Brayden.

One day at the dawn, Mr. Brayden hesitatingly enquired to Mr. Forge, " Sir, what was that great tragedy that vanished your all glory and prompted you to reside in this house far from the town"?

Mr. Forge smiled and gazed the clear sky for sometimes. His eyes were shining with the painful tears. Suddenly the pace of virile air increased and the cypress trees wagged fast.

Mr. Forge answered, " Whenever, I reminisce that tragedy, my eyes start draining and my old body becomes more fragile . Such a painful incident it was! "

8

LENVO'S MELODRAMA : PAST DOOMSDAY

Mr. Forge effused his heart to Mr. Brayden, " What a father wants from his son! Love, compassion and respect towards his parents! My only son was not opted with my kindness towards my country . He asked me numerous times to settle abroad leaving this old abode but I always forbade. I never wanted to leave my house as this house reminds me his shimmering childhood. But one day my son went abroad leaving me alone in this country in old age ".

Mr. Brayden, whose eyes were filled with tears, commended Mr. Forge who was weeping reminding his painful past incident.

Mr. Forge continued his story and uttered, " Since I had worked hard for the bright future of my country, the government of Switzerland has helped me a lot by providing me funds to sustain my life. But my heart cumbered with the profuse pain. One day at the time I was roaming in the jungle for the collection of firewoods, I saw a lonely boy convulsed the whole forest with its loud cry. A stupor stuck in my heart and I took him in my house when he confided that he had been alone in this world. Living with merriness, the admirable boy always aided me at every aspect of my life. I started finding the shadow of my son in the boy. He wittingly cleansed this house and this exceptional hoarding was also set up by him baptizing our house. But as the Sun has to set at last, the sunshine in my life also disappeared and left me at the shore of sea".

Mr. Brayden hesitated how.

Mr. Forge cried with a cumbered heart, " The boy died "!

He was languished that he had lost the ability to utter even a single word regarding the death of the boy, whom he had given a space in his heart . Mr. Brayden understood the profound pains of Mr. Forge and asked him to take rest for sometimes.

Hard and painful life of the owner of the abode afflicted Mr. Brayden who has confined the privy of Mr. Forge upto himself and not even iterated to Mr. Lenvo. The perseverance of Mr. Forge enriched the poise of Mr. Brayden to recondition the former's grevious life .

The stipend of Mr.Brayden was not enough to pay the rent to Mr. Forge. Despite asking for his arrears , he always avouched to Mr. Brayden, "Trust on the kindness of God Almighty! It will definitely enkindle the fused merriness in our life! So my beloved one! Extinguish the inner fire of paying my arrears. Let Mr. Lenvo find any job first. Then we will be balanced ".

Remarkable generosity of Mr. Forge sometimes vanished the dreams of Mr. Brayden and on that the propelled thought of unemployed Lenvo deserted his condition even more doleful. The anxious eyes of Mr. Brayden started to prospect some other kinds of jobs for his friend, Mr. Lenvo.

The felicity of Mr. Brayden touched the apex when his grim faith pleased and Mr. Lenvo was offered the job of an actor in a melodrama organized by English in the town. Acting in the play was an overwhelming will of Mr. Lenvo who was proved to be a good actor and was appointed for the protagonist of the melodrama after signing the agreements. Mr. Lenvo loved the job and felt contented and this satiated Mr. Brayden.

The peculiar melodrama , usually executed for forty days, was considered to be one of the most eminent plays coordinated by

English around the world. Rousing the most perilous and queer catastrophe, the English extirpated the golden rooted words of history of their country to demonstrate the richness of their immortal Lord to the world. Boundless reputation existed in the hearts of English for their Almighty Lord.

Mr. Lenvo tasted the gist of the play and overwhelmed to know the history of Earth. He used to iterate the past story to Mr. Brayden in nights when he was alone . Every day Mr. Lenvo came with the upcoming story of the melodrama and iterated to Mr. Brayden who also started taking the taste of past. The gist of the story was illustrated as,

Whenever the malignant perverts outlived on the Motherland pervading the forlorn air among individuals and she got cumbered with their offensive evils, the Lord resurrected at the requisite time smiting the restive tyrants and annihilating the blitz against humanity.

The same stunted time came many centuries before in England when the ruthless rogues had endeavoured to perish the humanness and the innocents with an incursion of deadly doomsday. And when the ruffians had bereaved the gladness of the country, then their deity reborn to retain the repute of the country victimising the multitude of miscreants.

The tongue of history iterated the past calamity that might have yelled doomsday for the demise of the motherland.

Proven by history, a statement illustrated that whenever a tied land had been flourished with an unleashed opulence of merriness and opals, the nefarious foes also had been emerged for the obsequies of blessings and harking the obituary of the thriving land.

The same crisis had been happened in England.

Many centuries before, it had been the days of spick brightness of the moon and snug sunshine of the sun. Sprawling on the streak of soil and springing under the spare sky and splattering on the sombre sea had sputtered the strenuous days of the past. Even the orisons of nonentities had echoed in the ears of God Almighty .

But the nights had been started quivering with the dreadful howling of wolves when the enemies of the country spurted and sprouted instantaneously. The splendour of England had not been tolerated by them. The foemen finally clinched to smother the opulence of the country to seek solace . A weird pandemic during past could be proven even more perilous. Inspite of that, the pestilence had been spread to smite the whole country . The widespread germs had pervaded it's hands on the whole country like the fierce forest fire.

9

CRYPTIC SOUND FROM HOUSE

The plan of the enemies of England had worked when the peril encircled the whole country. But the disease had spread so fast that it had even started ravaging the other countries also. The eyes of people of those times had prophesied an upcoming doomsday which would rip the heart of the Earth and devastate the human life.

The unbridled disease risen from England, had pervaded in the whole world and weaned the soul from the body. The trill of the Earth had been reverberating and eventually raised the Lord, Devin Drane for the existence of humanity.

Lord Devin Drane born in England, had relieved the whole world from the deadly disease by providing the salve of disease to everyone. So the whole world worshipped and revered the Lord and to sustain the prestige of their God, the English had been organising the melodrama every year in several countries .

These present untidy days of doomsday accepted the fact to upraise the past by reminiscing the history of Devin Drane . So there were numerous countries chosen by English where they were organising the melodrama to spill out the dread of doomsday from them.

Still the upcoming doomsday was in doubt of many people who imagined it just a fantasy or a means to dare the people on Earth. While on the other hand, many of the people feared from the approaching doomsday recognising it to be the day of the end of manhood from Earth.

It was the last week of February when doomsday was mere five months far to cease the throbs of thralls for ever. Mr. Brayden and Mr. Lenvo , farther from the affliction of doomsday, lived in sobriety in toto with the owner of the house, Mr. Forge and the speaking lark, Flen which has also started residing with them from the day it had met them in the train.

Mr. Brayden and Mr. Lenvo was always punctual and sincere towards their job. Mr. Forge handled the workouts of the house for the whole day and never left his abode lonely and Flen usually flied outside far to take the savour of Independence during the day time and came before both the men arrived from the town at nights.

Calmed the nature, the cypress trees revered with the mildly blowing zephyr in the replete aroma of ruddy flowers. Sand of wilderness washed in the ditch under the ocean of fragrance . In the cue of the picturesque moon, the raring water in the creek overflowed crossing the periphery and filled the perforations near it's shore.

When Mr. Brayden stood on the balcony sensing the soft puff of air on his body at night, he found himself sinking in the pure odor mingled in the air. On it the recalling of the past and his eccentric faults altered his overall mood. Anonymously an uncanny thought stuck in his mind about the connection between the prestige he had earned in London and the reputation Swiss had for Mr. Forge . Prolonged thinking on the qualms regarding the eeries behind this connexion between him and Mr. Forge took the soul of Mr. Brayden in a cryptic world. In the last, the sobriety of air terminated and Mr. Brayden's heart pulsated swiftly foretelling the prospect of an upcoming tremendous calamity in the life of Mr. Brayden.

Mr. Brayden grasped the throbs of his heart and remained firm for every prongs of his life. Ready to face every challenges of his life that the God Almighty had enumerated in the horoscope of Mr. Brayden, he got mused in the hypnotism of the overflowing air which touched his intrinsic heart and he closed his tearful eyes to beg for the morale to face the obstacles of his life. The undimmed Moon shone brightly to bless Mr. Brayden for the forthcoming tragedies in his life that could even be turned up obnoxious for the whole world.

Mr. Brayden at last went in his room.

The melodrama was only three weeks to end and Mr. Lenvo was eager to know how Lord Devin Drane had eventually salvaged the whole Earth. But the end would once again bring apprehension in the house regarding unemployed Mr. Lenvo. Palled by pleading several times by Mr. Lenvo to Mr. Forge to go to town and take a vista of the melodrama, but Mr. Forge always forbade consoling him that he never wanted to leave his house alone . It seemed the attachment he had with his house that his mellow heart had been resting beneath the house in a pall. Neither Mr. Brayden nor Mr. Lenvo had the power to snub whatever Mr. Forge iterated.

One night Mr. Brayden was thinking about the past that Mr. Forge saw him and soothed him alleviating his pains and his anxiousness to know the upcoming future.

After listening the modest voice of Mr. Forge , Mr. Brayden went to bed. Unable to meet the dreams, he resolved to traverse outside for few minutes in the refreshing air to take away the mind from distress to calmness. Quenched his thirst by drinking a glass of water, Mr. Brayden ajared the bedraggled wooden door of his room with a jerk. He went to the room of Mr. Lenvo and found him smiling in dreams . Glad to see the face and true humanness in Mr. Lenvo, Mr. Brayden decided not to quit trusting on him ever in the future . He alighted the ramshackle stairs and opened the main door. The environed coolness around absorbed the hotness of the wilderness. Mr. Brayden felt invigorated outside under the bright Moon.

Mr. Brayden sat under one of the evergreen cypress trees listening the rustling of the leaves calmly. The exquisite air flowed against his visage.

Abruptly, he heard the clatter of Mr. Forge echoing in the calm house. Mr. Brayden astounded getting the sudden stammering words of Mr. Forge. After harking the loud cry from the house, Mr. Brayden immediately stood up and hied towards the house to untangle the mystery behind the noise of Mr. Forge.

10
BEHIND THE GORY STILETTO

Avid eyes of Mr. Brayden saw the jagged door of the house. Mr. Brayden at once forcibly tugged the door and entered in the house. Astonished to see nothing in the hall, he planted the stairs to reach the room of Mr. Forge. He opened the door of the room of Mr. Forge and completely bewildered not able to find him there. Suddenly, a hand on the stiff shoulder of Mr. Brayden was quiet not abided by him and he turned back to see Mr. Lenvo . Mr. Brayden took a sigh of relief.

Enquiring about his condition, Mr. Lenvo asked him about the loud voice of Mr. Forge. Mr. Brayden striken with panic, held the hands of Mr. Lenvo and started prospecting Mr. Forge by shouting aloud hither and thither. Restless eyes of Mr. Lenvo roved in the whole house but sought noone. The zest to reveal the mystery of Mr. Brayden extempore was rising every second.

After searching the whole house, Mr. Brayden was not able to espy anyone other than him and Mr. Lenvo.

Mr. Brayden confided, " From the first day I came to this house my heart was beating telling that something mysterious had been hidden in this house and that is out of our reach ".

Mr. Lenvo damned, " Probably, it is Mr. Forge who is hiding something from our eyes. But what shall we do next, sir? "

Driven with fear, extemporeously, Mr. Brayden, a detective by profession, saw the worn out carpets of the open hall quivering with pain. He instantaneously stepped down the stairs and Mr. Lenvo chased him. Mr. Brayden at once heaved the dirty habiliments of the hall and both of men amazed to see a blonde coloured haze emerging from the wooden floor of the house and pointed towards the unleashed sky .

Mr. Lenvo fainted with the dreadful vista of the cryptic haze. Mr. Brayden braced him lying on the vacant land and ran towards the haze acknowledging it to be deeply mysterious.

He gazed the haze for long that his eyes amazed after abiding the weird scene of terrible haze and drowned in the whirlpool of tears.

Dismissing from the fervent core of the Earth and slashing the wooden land , the horrendous blonde coloured haze, veloce, treaded in the tremendous and limpid firmament. As the arrow leaves a bow, the vivid haze relinquished the cumbersome land pointing the dark sky. The grisly whinny of the detonation in the land rumbled the fledged soil lied on the floor .

A low sound during the ghastly twilight penetrated the soil echoed in the environed air. Jutted calmness outside droned in the lagoon of the squeak reverberated from the haze. Sparse twilight stifled the nebulous sky which was retrieved from it and curbed the sobriety which was clattering aloud to smother itself.

Sipping the fear, Mr. Brayden stood firmly in the fiasco of not been able to do anything. The cryptic haze scared Mr. Brayden much that even the sound of the splattering of the tiny drops of fright left him thunderstruck.

Immediately , the black sky started brightening giving a perilous vista of a gory stiletto. Abruptly, the blonde haze abandoning the wooden land congregated in the firmament and encircled the gory stiletto.Hemming the grievous stiletto, the stifled creak of the haze lowered adorning sobriety in the nature. Thrusted in an unleashed sea of mystery, the detective , haply, contemplated about the gruesome twilight and ruddy stiletto high in the dark sky.

Enter Caption

Switzerland was sleeping except Mr. Brayden and the gory stiletto which was circled with the blonde haze.

Among all the grave daggers and precarious stilettos, the environed one was the most perilous with the stern carvings of a horrid phantom followed by, abruptly, the casualties of mankind. It was drenched with scarlet veins ahead of the quaint carvings. The victims could be smitten with mere a single onslaught of the dagger with the acuate blades. Rain of blood was trickling on the wooden land from the ghastly dagger cleansing the silence of the ambience. From the abjectly motif of the gory stiletto, the fizzy drops of blood splattered on the wood and quenched the sanguinary land.

The treacherous mysticism and the raining of blood girded the brisk sapience of Mr. Brayden from the sturdy fetter of eeriness.

As Mr. Brayden spread on the soiled carpet on the wooden land to wipe the blood , the blonde haze vanished and the gory stiletto descended from the high firmament and got submerged in the wooden land. Infuriated with this, Mr. Brayden once again heaved the worn out carpet but amazed to see nothing there , neither the drained blood nor the gory stiletto.

Mr. Brayden stricken with fear, moved behind and saw Mr. Lenvo sleeping. He aroused him.

Mr. Lenvo rose and saw that Mr. Brayden was left in the mystic. Mr. Brayden's red eyes exemplified a brobdingnagian tragedy that was not feasible to illustrate in words and his shuddering heart feared that the gory stiletto was pursuing to victimize him for his past deeds. Mr. Lenvo corresponded that the past few minutes of the life of Mr. Brayden resulted tremendously queer that he was not in the condition to reveal the mystery behind the blonde haze.

So, Mr. Lenvo without enquiring anything, braced Mr. Brayden upto his room . Mr. Brayden shared the room with Mr. Lenvo so to cushion the fear for the dreads circulating in the eerie house.

Mr. Brayden was watching the same dreadful incident of night in his dreams. He eventually woke up when the horrid nightmare suddenly incited him to rise. He saw the clock resting beside Flen and it was happening six o' clock . Rubbed his eyes, the tragedy of following night again pecked in the mind of Mr. Brayden.

He first of all went to the room of Mr. Forge and astonished to find him sleeping . He aroused Mr. Lenvo and together they laid the conclusion to cognise the concealed mystry behind the old and ancient house of Mr. Forge.

11

CULPRIT AND SALVE OFDOOMSDAY

Mr. Brayden was still indebted of Mr. Forge, the owner of the abode, not only for arrears, but also for his assistances, nevertheless, he clinched to enquire about the mystery behind the blonde haze and gory stiletto to him.

The sunday morning tea ended .

Mr. Lenvo said to Mr. Brayden, " Friend, I have planned to go with Flen in the town. This will be considered the best time to enquire Mr. Forge about the mystery and eeriness residing in the abode .

Mr. Brayden nodded .

He asked Mr. Forge to go to the balcony to absorb some fresh air together.

In the balcony where cool breeze was blowing, Detective Mr. Brayden exaggerated Mr. Forge ," Huge respect resides in my heart for you, elder! Your lenient heart has jacked our words to thank you. It bloomed our lame and jittery life as , unfortunately, we had missed our expectations in the labyrinth before our perplexed eyes perceived the pleasure of your auspicious sight on us ".

Mr. Forge declaimed Mr. Brayden ," Don't ashame me! What I have done was to illustrate the souvenir of humanness on the Earth! On the other hand, I must thank to you to embellish my alone life again with the peals of laughter and decorous emotions ".

Mr. Brayden smiled and reiterated, " Thanks elder to give us such a huge repute! " and added that ," Elder! actually an unbearable question in my mind is pecking my tongue to ask to you from the yesterday night.

May I ask "?

Mr. Forge enquired, " What question , my son? "

Compelled to ask to unveil the enigma, Mr. Brayden dilly-dallied, " The day I came here, my mellow heart was pulsating shouting that there are some hidden mysteries in the house. But I ignored it. Yesterday night, I went outside to elapse few seconds in the calm nature for not being able to sleep, and when I came inside I was very astonished to see a blonde haze expelled from the land and glistened the sky. In the midst , a grave gory stiletto brightened from which blood was draining .

What is the eeriness behind it, Elder? Why do the cascades of blood splatter from the gory stiletto and quench the thirst of sanguinary land? "

Static Mr. Forge almost lost in another world, stood steep and mused after harking Mr. Brayden.

Mr. Brayden said in low voice, " Sir, I want the eeriness behind all these incidents. Sir, please, my steadfast ears are awaiting the reply ".

Tears in eyes, Mr. Forge answered , " My son! The bow of suspicion is right and this has opened the closed book of this mysterious house. I have scrutinised you the first day and your draining eyes for your past obliged me to accept you a pure hearted soul. You proved to be a sagacious and salient person.

But please, my boy , escape from the past and forget what has happened yesterday assuming it be a nightmare ".

Obdurate Mr. Brayden with an immediate reply, said, " How my honour! How can I bury the dreadful incident of night under the mute palls . I acknowledge your earnest nature. The exquisite owner! Please sate my rogation with your words "!

Mr. Forge replied entreating to Mr. Brayden , " My son! I deemed you much so I have lost the capability to conceal the truth. So I am confiding the eeriness conferring that you will confine it to yourself and not reveal to anyone , neither Flen nor Mr. Lenvo".
Mr. Brayden nodding complying him and was eager to know the mystery.

Mr. Forge revealed , " The blonde haze and the gory stiletto which you saw yesterday emerged from the cumbersome heart of a vengeful soul enveloped in a spacious sheet of soil terrifying the world with its squeal and scarlet tears that dashes and blooms its arid heart. The lavish pall stricken with a ponderous gash unfastened it's forlorn eyes in night whenever the pains of the buried pall under the wooden land exceeds and ripping the Earth , the twilight staggers the air and a gory stiletto brightens in the midst ".

Mr. Brayden investigated, " But sir, Whose martyr deepens with pain under the wooden land to glow the dark sky with tha haze ? And my humble elder, do you have any staple answer for the ponderous gash and the gory stiletto "?

Mr. Forge hesitated, " Any slender streak of my mind can not reveal about the ponderous gash as I mere once heard it from the boy who was living with me and unfortunately died .
And regarding the stiletto, I mere know that the intrinsic dagger is visible to only that person who is in the mission of stabbing the abominable doomsday ".

Mr. Forge again annunciated aloud," Mr. Brayden, God Almighty has chosen you the culprit as well as the salve of doomsday. You are the aide of this dismal world ".

Enter Caption

Mr. Brayden envisaged deeply whether his life was just an enigma inasmuch as becoming the cause of dreadful doomsday was a reprisal of the God for his unquiet mistake. On the other hand, becoming the salve to heal the dismayed world from the ghastly doomsday could be regarded as the benedictions of the Almighty for his stiff hard work to embellish the visages of the people of London.

With tears of morale in his red eyes, Mr. Brayden gasped and questioned Mr. Forge hesitantly, " Sir, then is it true that a person regarded as the culprit and salve of the doomsday can mere see the mystery "?
Mr. Forge responded," Yes, the dictum is true. Others who are in the betrayal to perceive it will be victimized by fainting them
or sometimes even killing them ".

Mr. Brayden thought that was the reason Mr. Lenvo fainted when the blonde haze expelled from the wooden land.

Mr. Forge ultimately confided placing his calm hands on the shoulders of Mr. Brayden, " My son! I want to reveal something more to you. Remember the past when I told you the story of a boy whom I found in the forest. He used to iterate a posy of considering the upcoming doomsday that

Merely the congregation of three weapons smite the doomsday ".

12
DOOMSDAY BY UNEARTHLY WORLD

The dictum about the doomsday and the undying eeriness along with the widespread rumour, impounded the candid mind of Mr. Brayden leaving him in the firmament of fiasco. He seemed the time , which was giggling on his faith, virile.

After hearing the profound mystery of the abode, Mr. Brayden was reminiscing about his eerie life . Mr. Brayden was totally rapt, inspite of that, he has not reciprocated the mysticism neither to Mr. Lenvo nor Flen . He had completely confined it to himself compling the humble orders of his Elder by not telling it to anyone on the Earth.

But, Mr. Brayden grasped that whatever the mystery hidden behind it, he would definitely have to constantly confront the horrendous peril till the date of the doomsday .

After returning from the town, Mr. Lenvo asked Mr. Brayden whether he enquired Mr. Forge about the mystery of the yesterday night.

Mr. Brayden avouched Mr. Lenvo, " Brother, I do not want to tell any lie to you. Mr. Forge has asked me to confine whatever he has told me regarding the mystic of the house to himself and I have promised to stand firm on it. So.. "

Mr. Lenvo acceded but asked Mr. Brayden, " Just a gist or a single clue will even satiate me ".

Mr. Brayden confided his friend Mr. Lenvo, " Grab it in your mind that the doomsday will emphatically knock the door of the world. And.. "

Infuriated with the upcoming doomsday, Mr. Lenvo asked , " And, what, Mr. Brayden "?
Mr. Brayden stammered, " And the cause... the cause... the cause of doomsday is me ".

Mr. Lenvo sank in the sea of affliction and abruptly fell on the couch as an arrow has assailed on his heart harking the delinquent words of Mr. Brayden. Mr. Brayden assured Mr. Lenvo not to worry about.
    Everything would happen as the God wishes.

Days passed.

Whose hue lured the dancing birds winging in the cloudy air and whose beauty oozed from the dainty heaven after blessed by the Lords , that nature started droning in the nought tardily. With this, the rustling of leaves was curtailed though the dry leaves of cypress trees splattered. The wail of dry trodden leaves fallen from the evergreen cypress trees arose to a greater extent than the whistling of fresh green leaves on the perennial trees. No senses furnished a gratifying reason of the abrupt alternation of overwhelming nature to a ruined one.

Afar from all the pains of nature, Mr. Brayden at nights glared the picturesque moon to bind himself in the orison to Lord whom he thought would aid him to withstand in every ordeal. Came to know that his life symbolised the life and death of the world, Mr. Brayden began dwelling mere for the sake of existing humanity .

Mr. Lenvo also at times reminisced the time when he had heard his God like Mr. Brayden as the cause of doomsday.

The days of the melodrama was also deducting . It was the last week of February .

It was the dark night when Mr. Brayden and Mr. Lenvo were arriving from the town performing their jobs and were only few miles to the home.

On the spur of the moment, a violent storm palpitated the roots of trees which quivered swiftly felling the leaves down on the worn out land. The throbs of the black sky was beating with the tumultuous ablaze thunderstorms which blasted to shudder the intense core of the Earth. Inundated rapids enraged with the storm and lightning, squelched the hindering rocks and drenched the wilderness drowning it in its ember. The ambience was trembling hiding under the lap of mother Earth. Resounding moans of dark clouds minced the sobriety when the heavy rain started flooding the whole world in water.

Mr. Brayden and Mr. Lenvo put their coat on head and scurried fast to reach their house alive. At once, the leg of Mr. Lenvo got stuck in the marsh which was swallowing it. Mr. Lenvo yelled for the help. Mr. Brayden backtracked to see the leg of Mr. Lenvo was almost engulfed in the enormous quagmire. He tugged Mr. Lenvo out and again hurried for the house placing their suitcase in front of the face to prevent the acute drops of rain and their coat on the head.

The visibility of the house enhanced and both of them eventually reached their house. The tatterdemalion door of the house was opened with a creak sound .

There stood a spacious and slender man whose emerald eyes were glinting to lighten the house. The dual faces of the amulet worn by the obsolete man visualised a pictorial vista of ogres sucking the veins of mankind. The hat he had worn doodled a painting of an occult scenery of sun glowing in the sky and at the same time, the firmament was glistened with the bright moon. Along with a queer ring painted with subtle colours in his fingers , he has worn the unusual apparels which prevailed him the Tzar of the World.

Both the friends astonished to see the guy.
Mr. Lenvo asked, " Who are you, friend? We have never seen you here ".

" Here my boys! The inkling of your arrival is echoing in the ambience outside. Let the chance rest on my shoulders to tell you some words about him " replied Mr. Forge in a loud and ghastly peal while descending the stairs and added," Meet him, he is Tzar Dray, my childhood comrade and the real owner of this abode and he wants to expel both of you from his house ".

Trembled to see his respected Mr. Forge , Mr. Brayden stammered, " Wh-wh-wh- Why, Elder " ?

Tzar Dray smiled and Mr. Forge confided laughing at the panic - struck visage of Mr. Brayden , " As you , the detective , have unwrapped each and every eeriness of our uncanny abode one by one, and now providing you shelter has become quiet perilous for us.

Moreover, from the day you came here, our task has been ceased also ".

Mr. Brayden inquired sedately, " Honoured Elder! I thought you to be a honest personality. But you deceived me! Well! What is your important task which my idle arrival has ceased " ?

Tzar Dray divulged in a loud sound , " The invention of the smearing pestilence in the world! A pestilence which will smother the pitcher withering the blossoming flowers. The humanity will be drown with the sudden flux of pandemic which will oblige the people wriggling with pain.

It will leave the sore demise of people the only way to get rid of the deadly doomsday. The real ointment will only be made in our heaven on the very afflictive day of doomsday when the moans of people wilt the blowing air " and eventually he screeched in a loud sound, "

FANTASM IN THE HEAVEN CREAKS THE CRAVING OF DOOMSDAY : THE SUDDEN OUTBREAK OF PESTILENCE
" .

Tzar Dray started laughing aloud and Mr. Forge followed.

Mr. Brayden considered Mr. Forge his doted Elder who would always be with him at every aspect of life. But, Mr. Forge betrayed him effacing the kindred with him for Tzar Dray.

Mr. Brayden and Mr. Lenvo was imprisoned in the cell of deceits by imposture Mr. Forge.

Mr. Lenvo asserted Mr. Brayden, " Sir! We must inform the whole world about the deceits of Mr. Forge whom people considered a trustee of Switzerland ".

Mr. Forge commenced laughing more loudly.

The irrevocable eyes of Mr. Brayden gyrated Mr. Forge and Tzar

Dray . His body was drenched with drops of sweat of suspicion on both comrades. Mr. Brayden gainsaid the idea of Mr. Lenvo.

Mr. Lenvo asked the reason behind being vacuous and not revealing the truth of doomsday to the world.

Mr. Brayden gasped and exclaimed with sorrow , " Since every human desires for life and never urges for death and whenever doomsday will come , everyone knows that even the cause of it will get ruined in it ".

Amazed with the swift mind of Mr. Brayden, Mr. Forge iterated, " I appreciate your fleet brain, detective Mr. Brayden ".

Mr. Lenvo was still dithered in the mesh of words knitted by Mr. Brayden.

Mr. Brayden literally stated promulgating in a mild tone , "Mr. Forge and Tzar Dray are not humans ".Tzar Dray hummed gibbering aloud, " Yea ! My boy! We are the Rex of phantom world . With whom you elapsed a month was not alive Mr. Forge but mere phantasm of Mr. Forge .

And now, just hark my words.

Only two options lies on your head now.

First : We have impounded your puny lark . If you will resolve to stay here , we will kill your best-loved lark and will imprison you both in the cell of the phantom world upto death.

Second : If you yourselves got expelled from my house, we will not interfere in your life ".

Mr. Brayden chose the second option inasmuch he did not want any impeccable lark killed due to his deeds.

Mr. Forge ascribed, " As your wish, But remember that you can save one but not the whole world .

Your lark is quivering with pain in the room. Take it and get lost in the world ".

Mr. Brayden and Mr. Lenvo planted the stairs hurriedly and found Flen trembling with fear and pain. They exchanged their story .

Now , the three friends were in the way to rescue from the demoniac house of Mr. Forge and Tzar Dray.

When they came back, Mr. Brayden saw only Mr. Forge. It seemed Tzar Dray went to his phantom world.

Mr. Forge screamed during the departure of Mr. Brayden and his two friends, "

SPECTRE PITCHER AWAITS WILTED VISAGES AND YOU - MR. BRAYDEN - CAUSE AND SALVE OF DOOMSDAY " .

The gist of the part two of this novel is illustrated below :

Part 2 describes the adventures of Mr. Brayden along with his two guys . After that , the journey towards the heaven was described .What they did after they have been dismiised from the house of Mr.Forge ? Will they reach the heaven of the phantom world to stab doomsday ? Is there any other doomsday ? Will the Earth devastate in the upcoming Doomsday?

www.ingramcontent.com/pod-product-compliance
Lightning Source LLC
Chambersburg PA
CBHW050811160726
48004CB00002B/788